This
Korky Paul
PICTURE BOOK
BELONGS TO:

blackbeth

georgia

Endpapers by Sujan Rai aged 10.
Thank you to Rose Hill Primary School, Oxford for helping with the endpapers.

For Carl and Kerri-Leigh – J.B.
For the Tzannes family – K.P.

OXFORD
UNIVERSITY PRESS

Great Clarendon Street, Oxford OX2 6DP
Oxford University Press is a department of the University of Oxford.
It furthers the University's objective of excellence in research, scholarship,
and education by publishing worldwide in

Oxford New York

Auckland Cape Town Dar es Salaam Hong Kong Karachi
Kuala Lumpur Madrid Melbourne Mexico City Nairobi
New Delhi Shanghai Taipei Toronto

With offices in

Argentina Austria Brazil Chile Czech Republic France Greece
Guatemala Hungary Italy Japan Poland Portugal Singapore
South Korea Switzerland Thailand Turkey Ukraine Vietnam

Oxford is a registered trade mark of Oxford University Press
in the UK and in certain other countries

First published 1991
First published in paperback 1992
Reissued with a new cover 2008
This Bookstart edition published in 2009

2 4 6 8 10 9 7 5 3 1

British Library Cataloguing in Publication Data
Data available

ISBN: 978-0-19-272958-3 (paperback)

Printed in China

Visit John Bush at www.storytimeafrica.com

www.korkypaul.com

The Fish Who Could Wish

Written by John Bush

OXFORD
UNIVERSITY PRESS

In the deep blue sea,
In the deep of the blue,
Swam a fish who could wish,
And each wish would come true.
Oh the fun that he had!
Oh the things he would do!
Just wishing away
In the deep water blue.

He wished for a castle.

He wished for a car.

He wished for a horse
And a Spanish guitar.
And he rode through the ocean
Singing 'O Solo Mio'
Backed by a group
Called The Hermit Crab Trio.

Once, when he wished
He could go out and ski
It snowed for a week
Under the sea.

He wished he could fly
And to his delight,
Flew twice round the world
In exactly one night!

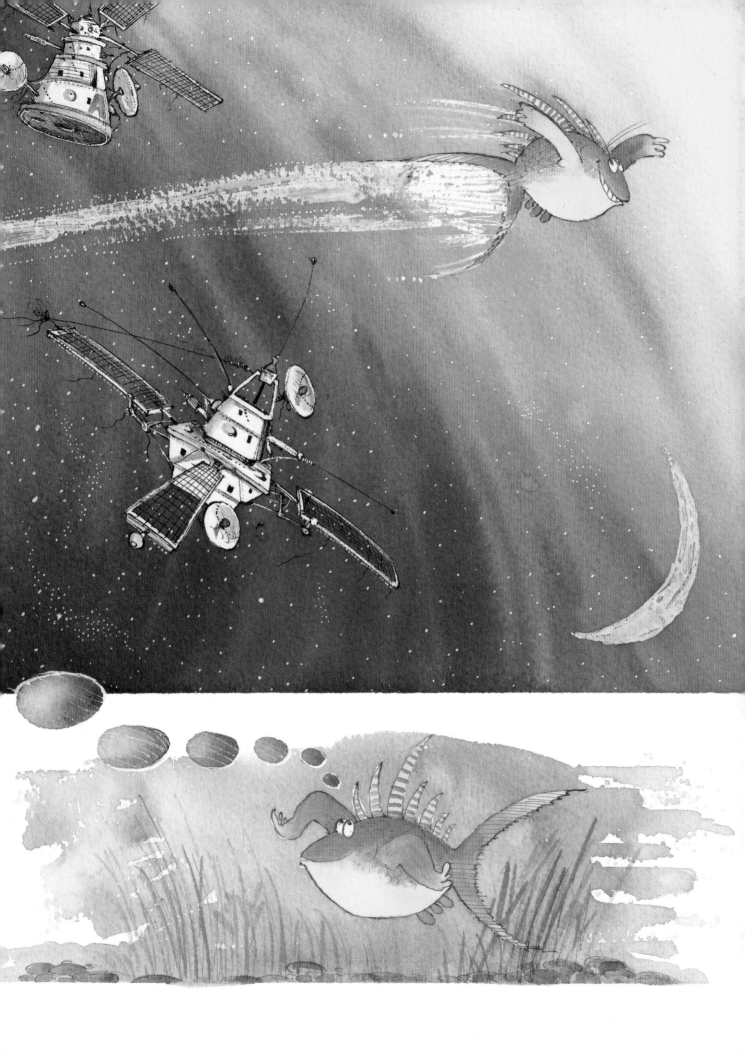

If sharks came a-hunting
For a nice fishy treat,
He'd quickly just wish
He was too small to eat.

And to teach sharks a lesson,
Do you know what he'd wish?
That he was a shark
And the shark was a fish!

He'd wish himself square,
Or round as a biscuit,
Triangular, oval . . .
Name it, he wished it.

He wished for fine suits
And handsome silk ties,
But the one thing he never wished
Was to be wise . . .

One day, just for fun,
That silly old fish
Wished the silliest, silliest
Wish he could wish.

That silly old fish
Wished he could be
Just like the other fish
There, in the sea.
But wishing was something
Other fish could not do.
So that was his very last
Wish that came true.

www.korkypaul.com